WHAT ON EARTH...?

WHAT ON EARTH...?

by Hazel Townson
Illustrated by Mary Rees

Little, Brown and Company
Boston Toronto London

For John and Vicky
— *H.T.*
For Granma
— *M.R.*

First North American Edition 1991
First published by Andersen Press Ltd.

ISBN 0-316-85138-8
Library of Congress Catalog Card Number 90-52937
Library of Congress Cataloging-in-Publication information is available.

Joy Street Books are published by Little, Brown and Company (Inc.)

10 9 8 7 6 5 4 3 2 1

Printed in Italy

"You go ahead and have a nice bath, dear," said Dad. "I'll keep an eye on Laura."

"Laura! What on earth do you think you're doing under the table?"

"Why on earth are you bouncing up and down on your mother's favorite chair?"

"What on earth do you think you're doing to the cat?"

"What on earth do you think you're doing with the garden hose?"

"What on earth do you think you're doing on the doormat?"

"Why on earth are you wearing your mother's winter coat?"

"What on earth do you think you're doing with my umbrella?"

"Where on earth do you think you're going with Grandpa's deck chair?"

"What on earth do you think you're doing with your sister's makeup?"

"What on earth do you think you're doing up on the wall?"

Just then Mom returned. "*What* have you two been doing? And…

where on earth is Laura?!"